A SCOOBY-RIFIC READER

BY GAIL HERMAN
ILLUSTRATED BY DUENDES DEL SUR

SCHOLASTIC INC.

New York   Toronto   London   Auckland   Sydney
Mexico City   New Delhi   Hong Kong   Buenos Aires

Map in the Mystery Machine, ISBN 0-439-16167-3, Copyright © 2000 by Hanna-Barbera. Designed by Mary Hall.

Disappearing Donuts, ISBN 0-439-16168-1, Copyright © 2000 by Hanna-Barbera. Designed by Mary Hall.

Howling on the Playground, ISBN 0-439-16169-X, Copyright © 2000 by Hanna-Barbera. Designed by Mary Hall.

Ghost in the Garden, ISBN 0-439-20226-4, Copyright © 2000 by Hanna-Barbera. Designed by Mary Hall.

Shiny Spooky Knights, ISBN 0-439-20227-2, Copyright © 2000 by Hanna-Barbera. Designed by Mary Hall.

The Mixed-Up Museum, ISBN 0-439-20228-0, Copyright © 2001 by Hanna-Barbera. Designed by Maria Stasavage.

12 11 10 9 8 7 6 5 4 3 2   5 6 7 8 9/0

Printed in Singapore   46
ISBN 0-681-15349-0
First compilation printing, January 2005

Scooby-Doo and his friends left Vinny's Pizza.

Velma, Fred, and Daphne waved good-bye to Vinny and his nephew, Joe.

Beep!

A delivery truck whizzed by.

Scooby dove under the Mystery
Machine.

"Rook!" he cried.

"It's a map!" Velma said.

The map was old and torn.

"It looks like a mystery," Fred said.

"It looks like an old pirate's map!" Velma said.

"Maybe the map will lead to a buried treasure!" said Daphne.

"Like, maybe we should not mess with a pirate's ghost," Shaggy said.

"Come on, gang!" Fred said. "We should check this out."

Fred followed the map.

He drove the van down a dirt road.

Screech!

Fred braked.

An old man stood in the way.

"Do not enter here!" the man shouted.
"This road is haunted! Turn back!"
"Good idea!" said Shaggy. "Let's go."
"Reah!" barked Scooby.
"Not so fast," Fred said.

Daphne and Fred and Velma wanted to explore.

"Let's split up," said Fred.

Shaggy and Scooby looked at each other.
To the left, the road was not so dark.
"Scooby and I will go left," Shaggy said.

Shaggy and Scooby took two steps.

"I think that's far enough," Shaggy said.

Then he cried, "Zoinks!"

Right in front of them stood a ghost.

"Ahhh!" shouted Shaggy.

"Rahhh!" shouted Scooby.

They raced down the road.
And there, up ahead, was a building.
A safe place!
Shaggy and Scooby dashed inside.

Scooby sniffed and grinned.
Shaggy's stomach rumbled.
It was a pizza kitchen!

"Rizza!" said Scooby.

What luck!

Scooby and Shaggy went to work —
rolling, tossing, slicing, dicing.

Pizza with everything on top — and everything all over!

Scooby threw the dough.

Up, down. Up, down, and . . .

"Roops!" said Scooby. "Rorry!"
The dough landed on Velma's head!
"What are you guys doing here?"
asked Shaggy.

"We followed the map," Daphne told him.

"It *is* a treasure map," Fred said.

"It is an ad for the Pizza Treasure Restaurant," Velma said.

"That's one mystery solved!" said
Shaggy. "But what about the other one?"

"The other one?" said Velma.

"The rhost!" Scooby cried.

"We saw it near the van," Shaggy explained.

"Hmmm," Velma said. "A ghost."
She took out a napkin.
"I found this on the road — right by the Mystery Machine. I have a hunch about this ghost."

"Time to set a trap!" said Fred.

Everyone turned to Scooby and Shaggy.

Scooby gulped.

"You want *us* to be the trap?" asked Shaggy.

Velma nodded.

"Ro way!" said Scooby.

"Not even for a Scooby Snack?" Daphne asked.

Scooby shook his head.

"What about two Scooby Snacks?" Velma asked.

"Rokay!" Scooby-Doo said.

Scooby and Shaggy walked down the spooky road.

"Scooby treats are just the beginning!" Shaggy told Scooby. "Soon we'll be eating pizza at Pizza Treasure!"

"Wooh!"

Zoinks! It was the ghost!

Scooby jumped into Shaggy's arms.
"Like, let's get out of here!" said
Shaggy.
In a flash, they raced away.
But the ghost was right behind them!

All at once, Shaggy tripped.

Bump! Scooby fell right on the ghost!

"Scooby-Dooby-Doo!" Scooby barked.

Velma, Fred, and Daphne ran over to see what happened.

"The costume party is over, ghost,"
said Velma.

Fred tore off the mask.

It was Joe, Vinny's nephew from
Vinny's Pizza!

"He's scaring people from this road," Fred explained. "Just like that old man said."

"He does not want anyone to go to Pizza Treasure," Daphne said.

"The napkin gave me the first clue," Velma added.

Shaggy looked at Joe, surprised.

"But, like, the pizza at Vinny's is great. We will never stop going there!"

"Really?" said Joe.

"Reah!" said Scooby.

"It is good to have two pizza places in town," Fred said.

"Like, then we can have a double order at two places," Shaggy said. He rubbed his rumbling stomach.

"Reah!" Scooby agreed. The gang followed Joe to Vinny's Pizza for an extra special pizza party.

"Rummy!"

Scooby-Doo rubbed his tummy and looked inside the donut store.

His friends looked too.

"Doodles Donuts!" Shaggy read the sign.

"Let's go inside!"

"Hi! I'm Dora," said the owner.
"Hello," said Fred. "I'm Fred and these are
my friends, Daphne, Velma, Shaggy, and
Scooby-Doo."

"We would like some donuts," said Shaggy.
"Rummy!" Scooby-Doo said. In a flash,
Shaggy and Scooby-Doo gobbled down
dozens of donuts.

Velma and Daphne laughed.

"Hey, leave some for us," Fred joked.

"Your dog sure loves donuts," Dora said. "Just like my doggie, Doodles." "I guess that's why you call the shop Doodles Donuts," Velma said.

A few days later, the gang came
back for more donuts.
But the shop looked different.
Dora was packing everything up!

She was closing Doodles Donuts! "I have a big problem," she told the gang. "Donuts have been disappearing."

Dora sighed. "Every night I put the donuts in a bin in the back room. And in the morning, the donuts are gone! Last night, I stayed late," Dora

said. "And I spotted a huge, scary creature covered with fur. It was digging around in the bin . . . eating my donuts!"

"A ronster?" Scooby asked.

"How can I stay open?" Dora asked. "The
monster will come back. And who knows
what could happen?"
Velma stepped forward.
"We'll help," Velma told Dora.

"We'll stay at the donut shop tonight," Fred said.
"We'll find out the truth about this monster," Daphne added.

"Stay in the shop tonight?" Shaggy shook his head.

"Ro way!" Scooby added.

"That goes double fudge donuts for me!" said Shaggy.

"Please stay," Dora begged. "You can have all the free donuts you can eat."

"Rokay!" Scooby agreed.

"That goes triple chocolate donuts for me!" said Shaggy.

That night, the gang stayed in the shop.
Scooby and Shaggy slurped down donut
after donut.
Finally Shaggy yawned. He was tired from
eating.

"We might as well hide now, good buddy," he told Scooby. They closed their eyes to nap. ROAR! A loud shriek woke them up!

Zoinks! It was awful!

"It's coming from the back room!" Velma said.

"Like, Scoob and I will explore the front,"
  Shaggy said.

Velma, Fred, and Daphne raced to the back room. Scooby and Shaggy slipped out the front.

It was dark. Shaggy could barely see.

"Scooby?" he whispered.

But Scooby was gone!

Shaggy had to find the rest of the gang.

He had to tell them Scooby had disappeared.

Shaggy gulped. He tiptoed around the side of the building.
All at once a giant, furry monster leaped out.

DOODLES DONUTS

"Monster!" Shaggy shouted. Somewhere he heard Scooby shout, "Ronster!"
The gang rushed over.
Velma turned on her flashlight.

Shaggy gazed at the big, furry creature.
Scooby gazed at the big, furry creature.
"Scooby?" said Shaggy.
"Raggy?" said Scooby.

"You each thought the other was the monster," Fred explained.

"It was so dark, you couldn't see," Daphne said.

"And that gives me an idea!" Velma exclaimed. "Come on! I know who the real monster is!"
She led the others out back.

"ROAR!" The shriek grew louder.
Then they saw it.
The monster.

Huge.

Furry.

Scary.

Velma switched on the floodlights.

"Roodles!" said Scooby.

"You're right," said Shaggy.

"It's Dora's dog, Doodles!" Daphne said.

The monster wasn't big or scary at all.

"What's going on?" asked Dora.
She had just come by to check on the gang.
"Doodles is the monster," Velma explained.

"The moonlight and shadows just made her look like a monster," Fred added.
"Good job!" said Dora. "Now I can keep my shop open. How can I thank you?"

The gang grinned. Scooby rubbed
his tummy.
"Keep making those donuts," Fred said.

"And we can keep eating donuts!" said
Shaggy.
"Scooby-Dooby-Doo!" Scooby barked.

Hammer, hammer. Bang, bang.
Scooby-Doo, Shaggy, and their friends
were building a playground.

Daphne's uncle gave the neighborhood
supplies to build a new playground.
The gang was helping out.
Shaggy banged at a nail.
"Oops!" Shaggy said to Scooby.
"Almost nailed you instead."

"Stop all this noise!" an old woman shouted. She rushed out from the house next door, and frowned at the gang. "What is going on here?"

"We are building a playground," Drew Zooka said. He was the person in charge. The woman scowled.

"Playgrounds are noisy! I don't want one here. I'll find a way to stop it. Or my name is not Edna Spring."

The next morning, the gang came back to work.

"We're not letting Edna Spring stop us!" said Drew.

"We need to start on the sandbox," he told the gang.

"Did someone say lunch box?" Shaggy asked.

"Let's take a lunch break," Shaggy told Scooby.

"Lunch?" said Drew. "But it's nine o'clock! And we have work to do!"

"No you don't!" Edna Spring walked up to the gang. "I'd stop building if I were you!"

"I know, I know." Drew Zooka sighed. "You don't want a playground here."

The old woman shook her head. "That's not it. Werewolves are haunting this place. I heard howling all night long. This is not the place for a playground."

"Werewolves?" Daphne asked.

"This sounds like a case for Mystery, Inc.!" Fred said.

"There is one way to find out about these werewolves," Velma said.

"There's a full moon tonight," Fred told the gang.

"We'll stay in the park tonight," Velma added. "And see if any werewolves come."

That night, the full moon rose over the park. Piles of wood cast strange shadows, and Shaggy felt scared. He waited a moment, but all was quiet.

"There's nothing going on here!" he said.
"Scoob, let's grab a late night snack and go
home!"

"Reah!" Scooby agreed.

"Not so fast!" said Velma.

"Would you stay for a Scooby Snack?" Daphne asked.

In a flash, Shaggy and Scooby gulped the treats.

"Still hungry!" said Shaggy. "Time to go!"

Awhooo! A howl echoed through the park.

"Is that your stomach grumbling, good buddy?" asked Shaggy.

Scooby shook his head. "Rope!"

Shaggy gulped. "Then it's the werewolves!" he cried.

Shaggy and Scooby jumped in fright.
They raced to the gate.
"Like I've had enough playtime
at this playground!" said Shaggy.
But a howling sound came from the gate.
"Rerewolf!" Scooby cried.

Scooby and Shaggy ran, with the werewolf right behind.

They raced around the swings.

"Ouch!" said Shaggy as one of the swings hit him in the head.

Aaa-oooooh! the werewolf howled.

Shaggy and Scooby raced up the slide, then slid down.

They couldn't get away!

"Scooby! Shaggy!" Velma called. "Stop
playing around!"

"Velma!" Shaggy cried. "Help!"

"Relp!" Scooby barked.

Shaggy saw a pile of sandbags for the sandbox.

"We can jump onto those," he told Scooby.

Scooby squeezed his eyes shut. "Rone," he counted. "Roo, ree."

"Jump!" shouted Shaggy.

They jumped onto the bags — and heard another howl.

"Like, it's the werewolf again!" Shaggy shouted.

But Scooby shook his head. Now that he was closer, he knew it wasn't a werewolf. It was more like . . .

"Ruppies!" he said.

"Puppies?" asked Shaggy.

Scooby nudged the bags. And there were four puppies, waiting to play.

Shaggy said, "Well, okay, Scoob.
You found some puppies. But what about
those werewolves?"

"Those *are* the werewolves," Velma said, walking up behind them.

"Don't you see?" Fred said. "They are howling because they are cold and hungry."

"More noise!" Edna Spring interrupted.

"Yes," said Drew Zooka, hurrying over.
"I came to check on things here. What's
going on?"

"Scooby found the werewolves," Velma explained.

Drew looked very surprised.

"But they're only puppies!" Daphne added.

"Puppies!" said Edna. "How sweet!"

"Redna's ruppies," Scooby said.

"Great idea!" said Velma.

"Edna, would you like to give these puppies a home?" Fred asked.

Edna smiled. "Would I ever! And you know what? A playground is a great place for puppies to play."

One week later, the playground was finished. Right in the middle stood a statue of Scooby and the puppies.

"I've named the puppies Daphne, Fred, Velma, and Shaggy," Edna told everyone. "Not Scooby?" asked Velma.

"There's only one Scooby-Doo!" Edna said.
"Scooby-Dooby-Doo!" Scooby howled.

Suddenly, the van went over a big bump.

"Oof!" said Shaggy.

"Roof!" said Scooby.

The Scooby Snacks flew right out the window.

"Ruh-roh!" Scooby cried.

The gang was out for a drive in the Mystery Machine.

"What a great day for a ride," Fred said.

"Especially when you have a box of Scooby Snacks," Shaggy added.

"Rats right, Raggy!" said Scooby-Doo, picking up the Snacks.

"Stop the van!" shouted Shaggy.

Screech! Fred stopped. He backed up.

CRUNCH! He ran over the Snacks!

"What are we going to do?" Shaggy moaned.

"Like, we're starving!"

"Look up ahead!" Velma pointed to a vegetable stand in front of a farm.

"Reggies?" Scooby shook his head. "Ruh-uh."

"Well, it's not hot dogs and french fries," Shaggy agreed. "But it is better than nothing."

Vegetables are good for you," Daphne said.
And they can be as crunchy as a Scooby
nack. How about some carrots?"
Rummy!" said Scooby.

"Sorry," said Farmer Fran. "I am all out of carrots. I have been for days now." As she spoke she looked over her shoulder. She seemed to be afraid.

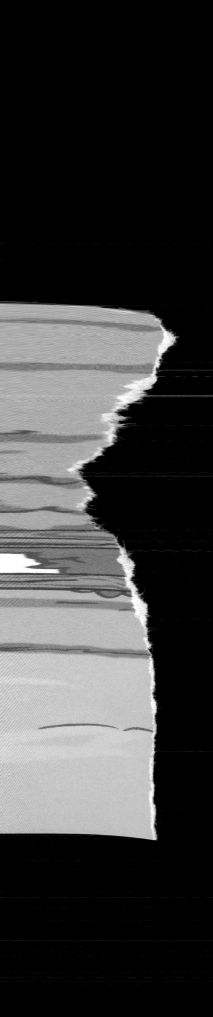

"Vegetables are good for you," Daphne said. "And they can be as crunchy as a Scooby Snack. How about some carrots?"

"Rummy!" said Scooby.

"Sorry," said Farmer Fran. "I am all out of carrots. I have been for days now." As she spoke she looked over her shoulder. She seemed to be afraid.

"Do you have anything else?" asked Shaggy. As he ran over to check the baskets, Scooby stepped on his foot.

"Ouch!" shouted Shaggy.

Farmer Fran jumped in the air. She was afraid.

"What's wrong?" Daphne asked the farmer.
Farmer Fran sighed. "Something is taking all
the carrots and lettuce.

Every night I hear strange sounds. And when I go to check, all I see is a flash of white. I am sure there is a ghost on the farm!"

"The ghost even chased away my farm animals! I am going to leave the farm and live in the city," Farmer Fran told the gang. "I do not want to go. But what can I do? I am afraid of ghosts!"

Velma walked over to the empty cages. "Hmmm," she said. "Mystery, Inc. will investigate the mystery! Right, Scooby?" "Ro ray!" he said, looking at the empty food baskets.

"Scoob's right on," Shaggy agreed. "We're not staying at a haunted farm. Especially when there isn't any food!"

"Oh, but there is," said Farmer Fran. "How about fresh blueberry pancakes for breakfast?"

"Rokay!" said Scooby.

But that night, Scooby and Shaggy almost changed their minds. The carrot patch was dark and scary. And there was nowhere to hide.

"Don't worry," said Velma. "I have an idea. You can dress as scarecrows!"

Farmer Fran brought big dark clothes and straw hats.
Shaggy and Scooby stuffed straw inside their jackets and pants.

"We'll be over there." Fred pointed to a big tree. "See you later!"

Shaggy and Scooby climbed onto the fence
posts.
At first, all was quiet.
"This is nice, good buddy," Shaggy said to
Scooby. "Nothing like a peaceful night in the
country."

Squawk! A bird landed on Scooby's shoulder.

"Rahhh!" shouted Scooby, frightened.

Shaggy laughed. "You are a scarecrow. The *bird* should be scared. Not you."

Just then a bird landed on Shaggy. "Ahh!" he shouted. Then another bird landed, then another and another.

Shaggy and Scooby shook their arms and legs. They shook their heads. The birds did not move.

All at once, they heard a rustling
sound. It was getting louder — and closer!

"Don't worry, Scoob," said Shaggy. "Nothing can get to us with these birds here."
Squawk! The birds took off.

Then Shaggy saw a flash of white — just like Farmer Fran had said.

"Okay!" Shaggy said. "This mystery is solved. There really is a ghost. Now, time for pancakes!"

He jumped off the post.
Scooby tried to jump off, too. But he was stuck!

"Relp!" cried Scooby. He saw the flash of white again. "The rhost!" yelled Scooby. It moved closer and closer to him.

Shaggy shook Scooby's post. He pulled on his paw. He yanked on his tail. But Scooby would not come down!

"That does it!" said Shaggy. He pushed
Scooby hard. Scooby's hat flew off his head.
It landed right on the ghost!

Then Scooby flew off. *Crash!* He fell to the ground, trapping the hat between his paws.

"Scooby has the ghost!" Shaggy shouted to
the others.
"That is no ghost," said Velma. She picked up
Scooby's hat. Under the hat was a small,
white rabbit.

"What's going on?" asked Farmer Fran. Then she saw the rabbit.
"Fluffy!"
"Your ghost is just a scared little bunny," said Velma.

"The lock on her cage was broken. So she just walked out," said Fred.

"And then she ate all the carrots and lettuce," added Daphne. "Fluffy was just hungry."

Farmer Fran laughed. She picked up her bunny. "How about a midnight snack?" she asked the gang.

Scooby licked his lips.

"Great!" said Shaggy. "Blueberry pancakes with whipped cream — here we come!"

"Scooby Dooby Doo!"

The Mystery Machine bumped along a dark, empty road.
Scooby-Doo and his friends bumped along, too.
"Like, we're in the middle of nowhere!" said Shaggy.
"I hope we have enough gas!"

All at once, the van stopped.

"Roh-oh!" said Scooby.

"Zoinks!" said Shaggy. "We *are* out of gas!"

"No," said Fred. He checked under the hood.

"Engine trouble. We have to call a tow truck."

Velma and Daphne looked around. Where could they find a telephone?

"Rook!" Scooby cried. He pointed down the road.

"I hope it's a house," Velma said, "so we can use the phone."

"And the fridge," Shaggy added.

The gang walked toward the light.
The light grew brighter.

They were getting closer.
Suddenly, Velma said, "Jinkies!
It's not a house. It's a castle!"

The castle looked spooky.
Scooby dug in his paws. He didn't
want to move.
"Come on, old buddy," Shaggy said.
"Think fridge!"
In a flash, Scooby swam across
the moat. He banged on the
drawbridge with his tail.

The drawbridge dropped.
Suits of armor stood at the door.
"Cool statues," said Shaggy.
Clank, clank. The helmets snapped open.
They weren't suits of armor. They were
knights. Shiny spooky knights!

"Who goes there?" one knight cried.
"Nobody," cried Shaggy. He and Scooby backed away.
"Come on," said Fred. "We have to find a phone."

Scooby shook his head. "Ro way."

"For a Scooby Snack?" Velma said.

Shaggy and Scooby raced inside.

Inside the castle, a chandelier swung back
and forth.

Creak, creak.

"That's funny," said Daphne. "There's no
breeze. What is making it move?"

"Rhosts!" Scooby whispered to Shaggy.

"Ghosts?" Shaggy said as a strange man rushed into the room.
The man opened his mouth to speak.
Scooby stared at his sharp, pointy teeth.
"Rangs!" said Scooby.
"He's a vampire!" Shaggy cried.

Shaggy and Scooby ran.
But the vampire ran, too.

"Like, since we're running," Shaggy said, "let's run to the kitchen."
"Reah!" said Scooby.

In the kitchen, they saw a woman. She stirred a giant pot that bubbled over a fire. "A witch!" cried Shaggy.

"You two are perfect!" said the witch.
"Just what I need."
"No way," said Shaggy. "We're not part
of your spooky recipe!"

Shaggy and Scooby raced away.
"Stop!" cried the witch.
"Stop!" cried the vampire.
They chased Shaggy and Scooby down
the stairs, to a dark, dark dungeon!

Shaggy and Scooby backed into the corner.

Suddenly, a mummy leaped up.

"Time is up!" he shouted.

"Our time is up, Scoob," Shaggy cried.

"We've got to get out of here!"

They raced up the stairs.
"Stop!" cried the mummy.
"Stop!" cried the witch.

"Stop!" cried the vampire.
"Let's find Velma, Fred, and Daphne. Then we'll get out of here," said Shaggy.

Finally, Shaggy flung open a door.
Down below, they saw monsters
and zombies and ghosts. . . .

And Velma, Daphne, and Fred!
A knight stood over them. He held
his sword tight.

"What should we do?"
Shaggy asked Scooby.
Just then the vampire,
witch, and mummy
leaped beside them.
"Rump!" said Scooby.

"Jump?" Shaggy yelled. Shaggy grabbed the chandelier.
Scooby grabbed Shaggy.
They swung across the room.

Shaggy and Scooby dropped to the floor —
right on top of the knight!
"My sword!" the knight cried.
"Grab it, Fred!" Shaggy shouted.
Fred scooped it up. But then he gave it
back to the knight!

Scooby hid his eyes. He was afraid to look. "Relax," Velma said. "The knight is going to cut the cake."

Velma stepped out of the way. Now Shaggy could see a party cake!

"It's a costume party!" Velma said.

"But," said Shaggy, "what about the ghostly chandelier?"

"I was pulling a string," said the vampire, "to move the chandelier into place."

"And the witch's potion?" Shaggy asked.

"Punch!" said the witch. "I wanted you to try it."

"And the mummy's warning, 'Time is up'?"
The mummy smiled. "My nap time was over!"
"But you chased us!" said Shaggy.
"Sure," said the vampire, "to invite you to
the party."

"Uh, we knew it all along, right, Scoob?"
said Shaggy. "We were just acting."
Scooby looked around at all the
smiling faces.
He stood up and bowed.
"Scooby-Dooby-Doo!"

"Would you like to use the phone now?" asked the knight.

"Uh, no rush," said Shaggy. "How about some cake?"

The Mystery Machine squealed to a stop.
Velma jumped out. "We are late!" she cried.
"The Museum of Natural History will close
before we get to see the dinosaurs."

"Scoob and I are sorry, Velma," Shaggy said. "But like, we *had* to stop for pizza."

"Don't worry, Velma," Daphne said. "There is time to see the new show."

Fred looked at a map. "The Great Dinosaur Hall is this way!"

"But the cafeteria is the other way!" said Shaggy.

Velma led the gang through the jungle room. Shaggy read a sign. "Gorillas in the Wild."

"Ratch out!" Scooby shouted. A gorilla was swinging right at them!

"Don't worry," said Velma. "These gorillas are puppets. They are wired to move and make noise so we can see how they live in a real jungle."

Shaggy sighed. "Like, I wish those bananas were real."

Next they came to the elephants. The animals raised their trunks. "Rakes?" asked Scooby. "Fakes!" said Velma.

"Even those peanuts!" said Shaggy.

Finally, they reached the Dinosaur Hall. Large dinosaur skeletons peered down at them. A crowd of people oohed and ahhed.

GREAT DINOSAUR HALL

"Look at that!" Velma said. "A real brachiosaur skeleton!"

"Amazing!" said Fred.

"Jeepers!" said Daphne.

"Rikes!" said Scooby.

The brachiosaur looked too real. Its great jaws opened and closed. "I am starving," Shaggy said.

"Re roo," said Scooby, licking his lips.

Shaggy turned to a security guard. "Like, where's the best place to chow down?" he asked.

"The cafeteria is this way," the guard said. He waved his arm, and hit a sign.

"Oops!" said the guard. "I have new glasses. And I still can't see very well. But I can take you to the cafeteria. I have to go that way to start closing the museum."

A few minutes later, Shaggy and Scooby had emptied the salad bar, the soda machines, and everything in between.

All at once, the cafeteria lights flickered.

On, off.

On, off.

Shouts echoed all around. Something was happening!

"Come on, Scoob!" shouted Shaggy. "We have to find the others!"

They raced back to the Dinosaur Hall. The brachiosaur skeleton swung its mighty head. It snapped its jaws. One leg moved, then another. "It is alive!" a boy shouted.

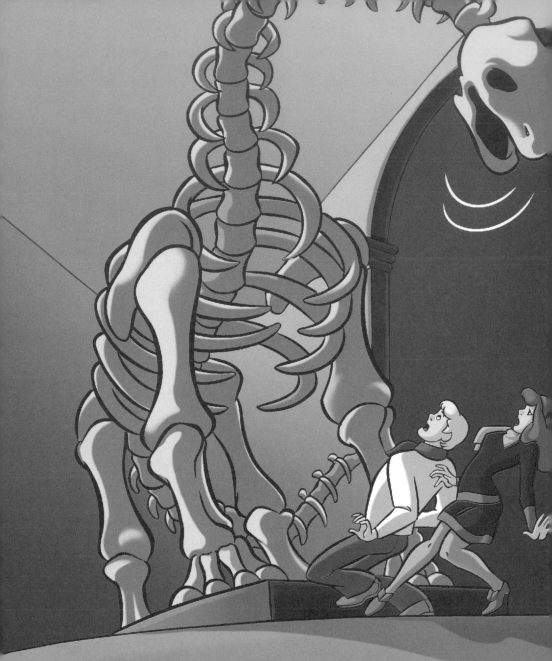

Everyone ran in fright. "Don't panic!" Velma
called.

A shadow fell over the gang. The dinosaur roared, right over their heads. "Run!" Fred said.

They raced past the elephants. The elephants raised their trunks and stomped their feet. They sounded angry.

Scooby and the gang sped past the gorillas.
The gorillas were swinging from vine to vine.

"Jinkies!" cried Velma. "What is going on here?"

"It looks like we have a mystery to solve," said Fred.

"But we can't hang around," said Shaggy. "It is closing time."

"Ret's ro!" Scooby agreed.

"Hmm," said Daphne. "Would you stay for a Scooby Snack?"

Awhooo! Howling filled the hall.

"Rikes!" cried Scooby, "a ronster." He jumped into Shaggy's arms.

"How about *two* Scooby Snacks?" asked Velma.

"Rokay!"

"Great," said Velma.

"Now, let's split up and look for clues," said Fred. "Daphne, Velma, and I will find the security guard. He might know something."

Scooby and Shaggy headed down a long, dark hall. With every footstep, they heard strange animal sounds. Then they heard a low, loud moan coming from behind a door. A sign on the door read KEEP OUT!

KEEP OU
MUSEUM
WORKERS
ONLY

"Zoinks! It is a scary jungle beast!"
Shaggy yelped.

"Ruh-roh!" Scooby barked. They raced back
the other way. They crashed right into Velma,
Fred, and Daphne.

Shaggy said, "There's a monster behind that
door! The sign says KEEP OUT! And, like,
that's what I want to do!"

"I have an idea," Velma said.

She flung open the door. Then she flipped on the light.

"Thank goodness!" said a voice.

"Hey, it's the security guard," said Shaggy.

"What are you doing here?"

The guard waved around the room. The gang saw buttons and levers and switches. "This is the museum control room," he explained.

"I thought so," said Velma. "I bet you stepped inside to close down the museum. But you could not see very well."

"I turned off the lights by accident," said the guard. "And when I tried to find the switch, I pressed all the wrong buttons."

"And everything went crazy!" Velma finished.
With some help from the gang, the guard
quickly fixed everything. The museum grew
quiet.

Then came a long, loud rumbling sound. Everyone jumped. "That's just Scooby's tummy!" said Shaggy. "Hey, can you flip one switch back on? The one for the cafeteria?" "Scooby Dooby Doo!" barked Scooby.